Sternberg was struck by tragedy in his teens (the passing of his two best friends) putting a dark full stop to his near perfect childhood. He sustained a grief-induced concussion and staggered into his future under its debilitating effects…. constructing a lifeboat out of humour he paddled on…

Sternberg lives with his wife of thirty years and their six children in Australia. Working the majority of his life as a janitor he also renovated a 90 year old haunted house, worked a 3 am shift at a chocolate factory, restored a jinxed 1968 station wagon, drove all over town to junior football matches and/or jazz ballet classes, ran a successful café for 9 years having little time for lunch or toilet breaks, became so tired he didn't know if he was awake or a sleep…and all the while writing little stories.

THE DISTINCT DISADVANTAGE OF BEING NORMAL

Allan Sternberg

To order extra copies or to
contact the author, please visit:
www.vividpublishing.com.au/sternberg

Copyright © 2019 Allan Sternberg

ISBN: 978-1-925846-95-9
Published by Vivid Publishing
A division of Fontaine Publishing Group
P.O. Box 948, Fremantle
Western Australia 6959
www.vividpublishing.com.au

 A catalogue record for this book is available from the National Library of Australia

All rights reserved. No part of this publication may be reproduced, stored in a retrieval system or transmitted in any form or by any means, electronic, mechanical, photocopying, recording or otherwise, without the prior written permission of the copyright holder.

*In memory of three great mates
that I lost, but never forgot,
Geoff, Gervase and Anthony.*

FOREWORD

Hammer Assault

In retrospect, my life has borne similar characteristics to being assaulted by a clawhammer wielding assailant. The blows never hurt so much at the time, due to shock and concussion, but the stunned moments that followed left me vulnerable to further ongoing blows.

I once read a quote from Hemingway who said, 'a man must take a lot of punishment before he can write a truly funny book', so for this next mile, here, pop my shoes on.

I was fourteen when I suffered the first blow. One Sunday afternoon my best friend took his own life; he was the same age as me. We had been through primary school together and were attending secondary school. Little did I understand that he was being bullied at school as well as at home. There were rumours of his suicide at school on the Monday but I was in disbelief;

it wasn't until later that afternoon when I saw his older sister walking up our driveway that it hit me. I remember turning to my mother and saying, "It's true."

Adding to that hit, my friend's sister told me that the last anyone saw of him that Sunday was when he was walking to my house to visit me. I was not home that Sunday afternoon; we were having a happy family excursion in the country as we often did. So my lonely friend saw no-one at my house, walked back home and ended his life.

How many times in my thoughts, dreams and nightmares do you think I walked home beside him that day? Only on those occasions *I am the ghost* and he cannot see me or hear my pleas.

So with no counselling (this was back in the "good old days") I was left to carry on. I had met a new friend at High School and he took me under his wing; he was tall, athletic and confident and I got a heck of a kick out of being his best friend. We shared the same interests and would sit and talk all recess and lunch time, just him and I. Sometimes we would kick a ball to one another joking and laughing. We took different paths and classes in the final year but still took time to catch up and discuss our future plans. On the final day of school he came with a group of his new friends to say farewell. I had an almost overwhelming urge to hug him and thank him for his support for which I was so grateful, but I didn't because that just wasn't done back then. Two weeks later he was killed in a car accident.

I didn't find out about the accident until the morning of his funeral. I was sleeping in when my mother woke me in tears. Within an hour of hearing of his death I was standing in a guard of honour of his school friends and sobbing as his casket was carried past me.

My other friends and I continued on into our lives and for the most part had a ball, but, of course, the memories of my lost friends never left me. Several years on, one of my closest friends at the time fell in with the wrong crowd and I turned my back on him. I wanted nothing to do with the 'wrong crowd' and often wondered whether I should try and persuade my wayward friend out of that situation. I never did and several months later he had a knife shoved into his chest and died that night.

We all make some decisions that turn out bad.

Midway through my third decade I found myself the father of no less than five healthy boys. One morning, out of nowhere, our four year old son became unwell and his health deteriorated rapidly over a two week period. He ended up at a major children's hospital located an hour drive from home. As his condition worsened he was moved to the Intensive Care Unit and onto life support as a 'precaution' the staff told me. Several hours later he was in an induced coma and the head surgeons of the Liver Transplant Unit came to assess my son. Having done that, they took me into a small meeting room and told me that my son was in the final stages of liver failure and his only hope was a liver transplant.

They then set about telling me the extremely slim

chance of an organ becoming available in the scant amount of time my son had left, a maximum of 48 hours. Even if they had an organ ready, there and then, there were tests that needed to be done and those results would take about that same time frame. What I had, they told me, was a very sick little boy who was in fact going to die. When they told me this in black and white they were probably surprised that I didn't crumble. It was a difficult thing for them to tell me, but I was steeling myself up for something much harder: I now had to tell my wife and my mother and the rest of my family that all idolised this handsome little boy.

Anyway, if you don't believe in miracles **then you should** because an organ became available, my son lived long enough for the tests to be done, the transplant was a success, and at the time of writing this he is a healthy strong young man pursuing his dreams. Look, things like this take the 'wind outta your sails' for sure but what else can you do but stagger on?

Everyone I talk to has had tragedy or trauma of some kind in their life, it would be a very rare person who has not, but what do you do with it? You can't dodge life when it wields it's hammer and I for one don't believe all things happen for a reason. I think it's up to us to make some sense and reasoning of events and you may find it takes most of your life to do so.

As a reaction to grief and trauma what I set about doing was to try and find the fun in things. Whatever the situation that presented itself, I looked for the fun. Not to be confused with 'making fun of everything' I still tried to show respect for people and situations, but if things weren't 'life and death' where was the harm in trying to have fun at the same time?

I felt I definitely needed to try and balance grief with light heartedness, with things that would really 'lighten my heart'.

I hope I have done my tragedies justice with the humorous stories that I conjured up to help light the dark times. Come with me now and let's have some heart-lightening fun.

Sternberg.

MY LIFE'S LIFE BOAT

All my timber is warping,
the colour fading fast.
Soon I'll have not one straight piece,
to use as keel or mast.

So as the tide goes rushing out
with everyone else afloat.
I will be left sitting on the shore,
in my feeble little boat.

                                        Sternberg.

'64 'VETTE

I was driving a 1964 Chevrolet Corvette in a hot rod race across America, as was the fad at the time. I was going great and in second place.

I had made the correct tyre choice, the gasoline I was using was premium extra leaded, and the crisp mountain air was making the huge V8 sing. Some hippies had given me pills that were letting me see the road uncoil in front of me in slow motion.

The gauges inside my brain read full revs.

My confidence was sky high. I had never felt so sure of myself in my entire life. "Yeah, I'm doing this baby, I can take this race. It's MINE!"

Up ahead I can see the leading car and I don't care what the Director said, when I get alongside Elvis I'm gunna sideswipe him over the cliff!

2 SEPARATE SITUATIONS

Isn't it amazing how long you can be stuck in a rut or slogging life out on the treadmill before you realise what your existence has become? It's not until some catalyst causes you to sit up and take a good look at yourself that you admit it is time for a change. That's what happened to me.

I become acutely aware that my life had splintered into two quite separate situations.

#1 …at work with its drudgery, boredom and repetition. I couldn't wait to knock off and get started on my hopes and dreams and 'escape projects.'

#2 …at home with its domestics trivialities, frustrations and the demands of my offspring. I looked forward to getting back to work so I could dream of getting started on my hopes and dreams and my 'escape projects.'

It wasn't until I was wearily riding my pushbike home from work one afternoon that my situation became apparent. The ride home was, thankfully, predominantly downhill and it was during a period of freewheeling that I happened to glance over to the opposite side of motorway and who should I see pushing their bike uphill on their way back to work? It was none other than ME. I am sure it was me because I sat up and had a real good look at myself. "Yep, there I go," I remember muttering.

I stared blankly at the road ahead and said aloud to myself,

"No wonder I'm so bloody tired!"

SHIPPING LANES

Most of the people that I knew and observed were just like me, going morbidly about their lives and waiting for their ship to come in. Somehow, though, I had mustered up the confidence to at last stop waiting and instead go **looking** for my ship.

I borrowed a little old fishing boat from Spencer Tracey's ghost and with my dressing gown tied up tightly against the cold sea breeze, I started on my journey.

I visited every far flung port and put in at many a small isolated fishing village at night but no-one had seen my ship.

Each morning I set off again, provisions restocked and confidence renewed, steadfastly sticking to the busy shipping lanes and keeping a careful vigil. Up until this point I had heard no reports of my ship being sited. Not one rumour of it in any smoky tavern, not a whisper in any misty port.

Until one sunny morning I chanced upon some old fishermen mending their nets on a stony beach. I stopped to have a pipe with them and they told me that 'yes' they had seen my ship.

They had seen it sailing aimlessly at night like some ghost ship under the moon. They had seen it labouring in heavy seas, beating into the wind. At other times it had been seen sailing around and around in dizzying circles as if caught in a giant whirlpool.

The following day I sat in my little boat drifting in the doldrums wondering how on earth I was meant to anticipate the course of a ship that was so obviously rudderless.

AS WINTER RECEDES

As winter recedes I find I am being woken earlier and earlier by both the morning light and the birds singing.

However, the other morning I was woken by the excited chatter of two tiny angels resting on the sun warmed bricks below my bedroom window. They were discussing the plans for some huge party, the invitations, how amazing it was going to be, the music, their costumes, the grandness of the venue and so on. They swooned at the thought of the guest of honour.

But it seemed that no-one knew of the exact date of the celebrations. Just then a cat scared the two little angels away and I have never seen them again or heard any more of this grand party.

I sometimes stand at my window, gaze out and wonder, "Will I get an invitation?"

CLAUDE

A rather intriguing looking gent was sitting on his own having coffee in a seedy, but arty, part of town that I love. I was overwhelmed by an urge to buy a cup of brew and ask to join him. Normally, I am way too timid for that type of social interaction.

Cup in hand I made my approach. The gentleman seemed somehow familiar. I was only two steps away when it dawned on me - this old guy was the spitting image of Claude Monet. I would use this as an ice breaker.

"May I join you Mr Monet?" I joked.

He spun toward me and eyed me with startled suspicion. I apologised for my forwardness and asked once more to join him.

"How did you know it was me?" he whispered, even though there was no-one to hear us. "Are you with the Arts in Time Program?" he asked.

Oh great, I thought to myself, this old bloke is a

dead-set looney. But no, it turned out that he actually **was** Claude Monet!

He explained to me that time travellers from the future had commissioned him to oversee the painting of a mural at the World's President's office in Bangladesh. (Bangladesh had become the world's super power and the President was based there.)

They had all been travelling back to France and the year 1866 to return him home when the time crew experienced problems with their reality stabilisers. They thought it prudent to stop now and let the stabilisers cool down.

Claude and I were having a delightful chat about Impressionism when two men showed up from the Arts in Time Program. They were dressed in a type of PVC their heads were shaven, and they had metal objects positioned about their faces. As a consequence, they were totally inconspicuous in this precinct.

It was time for Claude to leave. I leaned forward to shake his hand and was hastily warned not to touch Mr Monet, I was already in danger of suffering a disturbance in my own time equilibrium due to our meeting.

And then they were gone.

I was startled by the waiter alongside my table.

"My goodness" he gasped in delight, "is this yours?" He held up a paper serviette. On it was sketched an amazing impression of the surrounding street-scape. Monet's doodling! "Yes," I squealed "That is mine." I took it from him and placed it carefully into my jacket pocket.

My head was reeling, I now owned an original Monet, and I had spoken to him as he drew it. Thing was, I would never be able to tell anyone, or sell it.

"You are very good," the waiter praised me.

"A regular Rembrandt," he added as he walked back into the café with the used crockery.

"Monet." I corrected him.

"Yeah, whoever." came his reply.

EVOLUTIONARIES

A few of us more intelligent fish got our heads together and formed a secret group that we referred to as 'the school'.

We felt we had more to offer the world, and it more to us than just being fish, swimming about eating smaller fish and avoiding being eaten by bigger fish. No, we had bigger fish to fry. We called our school the 'EVOLUTIONARIES'. For we were sick of the cold wet ocean.

And one day we did it, we saw our chance and we took it. We all swam up to the beach and flopped out onto the wet sand, then onto the warm dry sand. We paused awhile to get our land legs then made for the cover of the beach grass, all except me.

I was mesmerised by the warm sand. I stayed behind and marvelled at the feel of it. I drew pictures in the sand, I built a sand castle, I dawdled about collecting shells. I came back to my castle and half buried myself in the dry sand, and in the sunshine fell asleep.

When at last I awoke it was night. The stars twinkled above me and strange night noises surrounded me. All my friends were long gone, so was the sun, and the sand had become cold. I had no choice but to dive back into the sea and swim beneath the waves. I took one last look at the beach in the moonlight and hoped my friends were safe.

And me, well, always the dreamer, I had missed my opportunity but I would bide my time for another chance.

SMOKING ON THE BEACH

The world was experiencing a time of great sanitation. Political correctness had been in vogue for decades, and now cleaning up and cleaning out society was on in earnest. Rightly or wrongly smokers bore the brunt.
Many smokers had "the earth is flat" mentality when it came to the idea of no smoking in bars and restaurants and would laugh and cough at the notion. But it happened. Eventually the future overtakes us all.
The beach front was next. No smoking on the shore.
For years no-one had been allowed to let their dogs poop on the sand. Now it was the smokers turn.
There was now no smoking at the football or cinema nor eating houses, drinking houses, gambling houses or toilets.
It was while discussing the smoking issue with some other male friends of mine who are still of child-making age, that I learned that new fathers were still permitted

to hand out, and smoke, cigars, either in the birth room or any other area designated to be in the confines of the maternity ward.

Thank goodness the world had not yet gone completely mad.

SPACE SHIP BOGEY

I once went to bed in the late afternoon in an attempt to repay my ever-increasing sleep debt. As I lay there in a tired stupor a blow fly was flying around and around my bedroom in a sort of holding pattern like a tiny passenger jet. Or was it a fly? I questioned myself. Perhaps it could have been some strange tiny alien spacecraft. Moments later a swoon overtook me and I fell into a deep slumber.

"I roused several hours later troubled by my index finger probing my right nostril. I became aware of an object that felt foreign to my normal nose objects. I sat bolt upright and pursued the object further in a slight state of panic, could the object be the space ship from earlier in the evening? And what the hell was it doing up my nose? Was it on it's way to my brain to steal my plans and ideas? And now I had inadvertently helped it on beyond the reach of my finger!

I fumbled through my bedside cupboard for a sock

and some insulation tape; I taped the sock over my nose and mouth. My plan was this-: The space craft would surely try to leave before morning after transcribing all my ideas and plans but while endeavouring to escape it would become confounded in my sock.

My wife woke me in the morning and demanded to know about the sock. I explained how the night had gone. She bellowed at me that I was an idiot and insisted that I remove the sock at once, turn it inside out and see that there was no space ship, then she left the room.

I studied every inch of that sock in bitter disappointment. There was nothing to be found, nothing except a two-inch cut too neat to be a tear and while I can't claim to be an expert it appears to have been made with a laser or indeed an ion blaster!

Oh, how I wish I had caught that little space ship so I could have shown it to everyone and used it to prove I am not an idiot.

URBAN WORRIER

During my existence as an 'Urban Worrier' I would read several newspapers that reported on cost of living increases. They would give opinions, reasons and causes of the upswings and predictions of the consequences.

Until one morning as I was seated on my own at the breakfast table an angel appeared and handed me a copy of the 'Angel News Pictorial', the smallest newspaper I had ever seen. In it's financial section it claimed that the cost of living was in fact static and had been for a considerable amount of time.

It quoted that the cost of tickling your children had not increased since Adam was a pup. And while the price of a bottle of red wine had increased, the cost of **sharing** a bottle with an old friend and having a good cry had not.

Sunsets and thunder storms could still be viewed at the same old rate as could full moons and camp fires. So it seems the cost of living, I mean **really living** had not increased one iota.

AUDIBLE PLEAS

"Despite my constant and very audible pleas for clemency, the antics of my assailants continued on quite unabated!"

Sternberg.

BOVINE REVOLUTION

Via a chain of events that I now find hazy to recall, I found myself Grand Emperor of the known world.

Here at last was my chance to halt the industrial Revolution of which I was not a huge fan. I reintroduced the one-acre-one-cow policy on a global scale.

Seminars were conducted on animal husbandry, as were handyman classes on constructing quaint rustic cow sheds.

Soon everyone was appreciating the importance of meadow grasses and clover flowers. Bees were befriended and nurtured.

Before sunrise, and at dusk, the planet reverberated to the sounds of 'calling in the cows'.

From my Imperial Palace I gazed upon my Bovine Revolution, had a glass of warm milk, and hopped into bed.

COMFORT ZONE

Among the most uncomfortable moments of my life (apart from wearing that mustard coloured hessian skivvy of my youth, the one with the corrugated cardboard neck tag and wire staples for stitching) is when people find out that I have an artistic bent.

"Oh, what sort of artwork do you do?" they will enquire of me, and I stutter and stammer for an answer.

I reply with one or two-word sentences. I look around for support from people who are not there. I make confusing gestures with my hands. I cough and swallow hard.

It is about at this point that they come to the conclusion that I am, in fact, a janitor.

HOW DISAPPOINTING

"How disappointing would it be to be granted your place in heaven only to find it inundated with pesky fly ghosts?"

Sternberg.

DEAR ENEMY

Dear Enemy,

I am writing on behalf of a few of our lads on the front line to express concern over what is, in their opinion, your heavy-handed use of artillery fire.

(I hasten to point out of course that this is **their opinion** and not necessarily that of us here at the war office.)

And while not wishing to inflame the situation in any way, I should point out that if our boys believe the current trend not to ease significantly, then we shall look into the viability of purchasing some artillery of our own!

(To this end could you recommend a trustworthy, reasonably priced supplier?)

Wishing you well with all your future endeavours,

                                                The Colonel.

ANTS

We all seemed to spot the ant simultaneously, our little group making its way to the steps of our favourite old pub. We stood over it in awe. That little ant was making its way along carrying an enormous bread crumb. We were all truly amazed. Here was one of God's little creatures, seemingly made of nothing, that was quite willing and able to transport a weight far greater than itself for who knows how far? We all shook our heads in disbelief, then I stepped on it and we all continued into the bar.

A few drinks later I was pondering my callous act and what ramifications there may have been in the ant world. I couldn't help but think that in a hole in the ground, not too far away, there may have been a large family of ants all sitting around concerned and glum saying to one another, "If that bloody caterer doesn't show up soon, the whole night's going to be ruined!"

GEOGRAPHY NEWS

From the television in the next room a news report really caught my ear. "Huge ground-breaking event in the World of Geography."

Geography is most uncommon in mainstream news articles, so I hurried to the glow of the set to hear more.

Apparently, two amateur surveyors had stumbled across a previously unknown country north of Bolivia's northern border with Brazil.

A huge thriving country, with a healthy economy and infrastructure, industries and agriculture, a country that no one had known about for centuries.

You can well imagine the finger pointing that ensued. Map makers, professional surveyors, ex – explorers and historians all blaming each other for the oversight. World heads of state embarrassed. Presidents demanding shake-ups of their staff in foreign affairs.

An honest-to-gosh ground-breaking event in the history of world geography. And the name of that new country, situated between Brazil and Bolivia? It's called Make Bolivia!

HEART BURN

"Owing in large part to that aromatic and pungent African voodoo cuisine, I now find I am suffering a most apocalyptic reflux!"

Sternberg.

STRINGER

Bloke down our way has had it rough, has had for most of his life I suspect; he has a disability. I don't know if he was born like that or whether he acquired it later in life; no-one likes to ask.

You always see him getting about and you do feel sorry for him. He can't do anything by himself. Poor bloke needs a helper to do everything, things that you and I take for granted. For you see he's a marionette, made entirely of wood with strings and all.

What amazes everyone is that he always has a smile on his face! His cheeks are rosy red and his complexion has a lustre that is thought to be polyurethane-based. I don't know his real name, everybody calls him Stringer, and he doesn't seem to mind.

Something happened to Stringer one night that changed us all forever, Stringer more so. Somehow, he came to life and became a real man! (Something I felt I had not yet become myself.)

No one knows exactly what happened but there he was all flesh and blood, no strings attached. I don't know what treatment Stringer was receiving, if any; maybe he was relying on the power of the written word and was studying, with dedication, some self-help guru. Who knows?

People in our street decided to hold a 'Coming to Life Party' for him. I went along but I felt strange about it. At the party everyone was happy for Stringer. I appeared happy too but I'm not sure how I felt inside. Look, Stringer had come to life and good for him, it's just that I had been alive all my life and I still didn't feel I had anything to celebrate.

Life for me had been bloody hard work with only frustration, disappointment and exhaustion to show for it. So I celebrated with everyone else but my heart just wasn't in it, the party lights were on but I wasn't home.

Maybe I was resentful because I had never had the opportunity to rise triumphantly from being made of wood and then miraculously become fleshed out. Nor had I risen from the ashes of some real calamity to an exalted plain of happiness.

No, I had to live my life held back by the distinct disadvantage of being normal.

ART SAW

It was my job to operate the art saw.
It was a dirty great machine that looked quite complex but in reality, you could have trained a monkey to use it. Sometimes, hungover on a Monday morning, I wished I had been the owner of just such a primate.
The art saw had many blades and would cut, shred, pulverise and mulch. It was my duty to cut up all the art that was delivered by semi-trailer each night. All the art that people didn't like or understand. Art that the people thought the government had paid too much money for.
Confusing art, confronting art, rude art, way-too-colourful art, offensive art and stupid art. Any art that 'my four year old could do better than.'
Cut, cut, cut. Mulch, mulch, mulch.
One morning two women showed up at the saw yard claiming to be artists. They collected a heap of art mulch

and told me they were going to use it to make art mulch mache sculptures.

The women were very excited but as I watched them pulling out of the yard I thought to myself: "Those sculptures are going to be buggers of things to cut up".

WAKING UP IS HARD TO DO

Normally I am not a fan of waking up because I find it raises more questions than it answers, things like: What will I wear? What will I eat? Why should I bother, and, who will be the first person to piss me off?

But I think today could be different!

Today I have woken up and the world around me has turned to wood. Hard wood, of good quality, hard but not uncomfortable. It's lined too. Lined and padded with a little pillow for my head.

And what's this? Instead of my rancid old pyjamas I have woken wearing a stylish new suit with a flower in my lapel. In fact, there is an over whelming smell of flowers. And soft music and... uh oh.

FINE LINER

My children had started to come home from school despondent. As their father it appeared that my zany antics were causing them to suffer ridicule and scorn.

I bolstered their self-esteem by prompting them to reply to their decriers with this retort:

"There is a fine line between madness and genius and one day soon our father may just cross over it!"

BAD JOB

My friend was intrigued to learn from me that I once held the job of packing up the sea for the night (known as Tiding). It was a lousy job and I only endured it for two weeks before quitting.

Each afternoon I would motor out in an aluminium punt to a large shed on stilts just over the horizon from the coast.

I would then proceed to fill up large tins with the water from the sea and stack them in the shed. It was hot, heavy work with no time for breaks.

A lot of tins had lids that were rusted tight due to the salty water, and as I was in a hurry, I would put these aside until later. Of course, this was a stupid mistake as it meant that towards the end of my shift all the lids would be hard to get off. As I worked the sea level fell exposing smelly salty mud. I would be sweaty, wringing wet, dog tired and now having to wrestle with the most difficult lids that were also covered in barnacles!

It seemed that no sooner had I packed up the sea for the night than it would be time to empty the water back out for high tide and stow all the empty drums back into the shed.

At last I would motor the little punt back to the pier.

People there would enquire as to whether I had caught anything. I would just shake my weary head and think to myself, "I'm not a fisherman you fool, I pack the sea away for the night."

WHAT STINKS?

The King sent me with a band of good men into the world to find out "what stinks?"

We rode past an old beggar woman, we rode past where the poor people washed. We rode beside the factory swamp. We camped beside a chicken coop. We rode past road kill. We rode through a moose graveyard.

Yorrickson's horse stood in something and my horse flicked up something else. We rode past where the big pipe emptied into the sea. We rode for miles behind a pig truck and camped behind the abattoir where, around the fire that night, we all agreed that working for the King stinks!

HOW TO STAY IN LOVE

"Share the weight of the lantern of love, hold it high to light your way.

Hold each other as you sleep and listen to the lullabies of angels.

Nourish each others hearts with conversation and honest tears.

And always go outside to fart."

Sternberg.

BITTER APPLES
(A BEDTIME STORY)

My younger brother woke me to the grainy darkness of our shared bedroom. "Look at the moonlight coming in through the curtains," he urged me.

In the gloominess of our room everything seemed to be black, grey or silver as the stark moonlight shone through the curtains. What my brother wanted me to see was the bizarre shape the moonlight made as it landed on the carpet. The pattern and gape of the curtains combined to allow the moonlight to spill onto the carpet and appear to be the evil insignia of some vile secret death squad.

I was not angry that my little brother had woken me to the freezing night, as I would have hated to miss this strange and eerie phenomenon. We stood together shivering and peered out the curtains at the moon with its idiot face grinning back at us.

My brother got back into his bed and was asleep within minutes. I, on the other hand, lay awake for hours. I could not get warm again nor could I get the evil pattern of the moonlight out of my thoughts.

It bothered me a little that my brother, so much younger than I, should know that I would be interested in seeing the moonlight, the moonlight that we could have quite easily missed as we slept.

What also bothered me was that old apple tree outside our bedroom. In summer the fruit was far too bitter to eat and in winter the gnarly old diseased branches would scratch and tap against the wall.

I was at an age then that I should not have been spooked by the tree's form and the sinister shadows it created at night.

However it was difficult not to be spooked, as even during the daylight hours I could clearly see one of the ghosts from my nightmares ensnared in its evil branches. My mother tried to convince me of course that it was no such thing and that it was merely a painter's flimsy plastic drop sheet that had blown into the tree.

I was having none of it.

CYBER LEAP OF FAITH

More than twenty years after Time magazine named a computer as man of the year, I began using one to write with. (A computer that is, not a man.) I was very reluctant at first but I soon became impressed with how time-saving and far less messy it was compared to the way I used to write.

In my old days I used to write in the very traditional manner, even going to the trouble of preparing my own ink from the blackberries that grew at the dangerous end of the woods. They grew in entangled groves along a cold and fast-flowing mountain stream.

The best time to harvest the blackberries was late in the season when the fruit was very ripe. Unfortunately, at this time of the year the bushes were full of hornets' nests and the hornets were all angry from the heat of summer. As I picked the fruit, the thorns and prickles would tear and pull at my legs, and the hornets would sting me up and down my arms.

Hornets' stings and bramble thorns were of course nothing compared to the injuries I risked from tangling with the angry bears that infested those woods. The bears would compete with me for the blackberries, which they also liked to feast on after the salmon run had finished. I used to smear myself with hot bear droppings that I found on the forest floor, that way if a bear caught a whiff of me it would think, "Oh, someone has already been over there".

Eventually, I would retreat to the sanctuary of the lower canopy of plants and, hidden away there, I would take out my mortar and pestle, and begin grinding down the meagre amount of berries contained in my picking can, having spilt many as I ran from the bears.

The berries needed to be processed as soon after harvesting as possible and slightly diluted with cold water from the stream. Once the proper consistency had been reached I would decant the ink into my dark blue ink pot, secure the cork and wrap it tightly in cloth.

With the ink jar safely in my old rucksack I would make a break for it down the track that led toward home, a mob of angry bears at my hind.

ATOMIC TESTING

Once when I was working as part of an atomic bomb testing unit for a country I cannot name, for security reasons, I received a scathing letter.

The letter was from a neighbouring country, which again I cannot mention, for those same security reasons. But I can reveal the essence of the correspondence which can be pretty much summed up with one line.

"HEY, KEEP THE FREAKIN' NOISE DOWN!"

ESCAPE POD

Sleep had not been the usual sanctuary of peace, calm and serenity that it had been in my carefree youth. Way back then my comfy single bed was like an escape pod that would jettison me each night into a surreal dreamscape, a release from any troubles, hardships or problems.

But lately, sleep and dreams had become as frustrating and exhausting as the prickles and thorns of my waking days. Any undertakings I took on in dream time always became just as entangled and hopeless as workplace dilemmas and the frustrated workings of our family life.

In one particular dream I found myself helping the road crew repairing the street in front of my house; I had the task of pushing the wheelbarrow of wet sand up the incline toward the repair site. The crew had given me a pair of overalls to wear but they were still damp from the washing machine. I sat them in the barrow on top of the sand but they kept sliding off every twenty paces or so. I had to stop and catch them, place them back on top and push on, having lost all of my momentum. I had delivered several loads before questioning "Why do I have to help repair the stinking road?" I let the barrow fall over and ran off. Moments later my alarm clock sounded and I was off to my real job already exhausted from my road repairs.

I now approached my bed with trepidation. Where the hell was it to take me this time, to what ridiculous assignment? To move a piano shaped refrigerator that was full of house bricks? And I bet I couldn't remove the bricks first as they will be wedged in too tight, and how many flights of stairs? A square wheeled trolley with the brake stuck on? And no doubt the overalls will still be damp from last night!

CHIMP CHATTERINGS

Everyone's mouth was agape when monkeys started talking.

It pretty much started when a huge gorilla made its own dental appointment. After that the monkeys really opened up to us and the more they told us the more we gaped.

According to them, primates were the first out of the trees and were prepared to make a real go of it; they colonized small pockets of the planet and for a while they thrived.

They told us they had a good thing going for a while and invented many a time and labour saving device. But with more and more time on their hands they started to become dumber and dumber as they spent their leisure time submersed in popular culture for the masses.

Their offspring became fat and lazy dullards, sleeping in late and hardly ever working. There was little need for working anyhow as most things could be got by way of a comfortable welfare system.

As time went by apes were talking to each other less and less as they preferred their toys and computers. Soon they lost the ability to talk altogether and not long after this everything they had achieved came crashing down.

They told us that during their time they had seen us emerge and grow, but they refused to tell us where we had come from, "Trust us, you don't want to know and we may have already said too much."

Too much indeed, we were speechless! This was earth shattering news to us, not that the earth did shatter, our little planet kept on turning silently in space.

Only perhaps even more silently now. It was silent at every point of the compass, at every corner of the globe.

You could have heard a pin drop!

Actually, you could have heard a used banana skin fall into a cardboard box full of moist ape droppings.

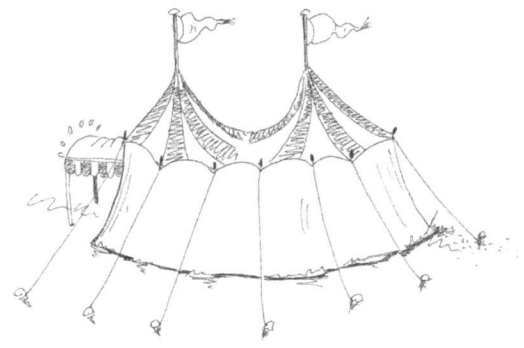

CIRCUS TENT

Growing up I was well aware that I was a weird and bizarre person. Little did I know I would grow up and out of it.

For example, as a kid at the circus I wasn't spellbound by the colour, movement and pomp. I crawled beneath the seats and out under the tent wall. I much preferred to wander the circus back lot and feed the elephants carrot weed, look under the caravans where the animals slept and peer into the vans where the performers slept. You could scarcely tell the difference!

I loved the dizzying surreal feeling of being in the sun smelling the dung, walking the seedy surrounds while in the big top the audience clapped and cheered.

Moments before intermission I would take a pee in broad daylight out in the open. In a few quick moments a hundred people would be milling around the exact same spot. I would blend in and disappear. I remember wondering, would there be opportunities like this as an adult?

SCHOOL REUNION

Why the hell I even went along to the school reunion I do not know, I usually shy away from those sorts of social gatherings. I guess I was morbidly curious to see what assortment of fates had befallen my former class members. The guys I had fought with, the girls I had fancied. The people who had voted me, in the final year book, 'the most likely to succeed.'

I watched them all pull up to the hall in their fancy cars dressed in their new clean clothes. Yeah, I remembered each and every one of them for sure. No one recognised me though, thanks to my drastic hair loss and stooping posture.

All night I moved around the old school hall like a ghost, listening to conversations but taking part in none. For the entire evening I was not offered one handshake, dance, cocktail or job offer.

Toward the very end of the evening I was offered

some left over food and several rides home in a car on account of the rain. I declined them all as I was happy to walk, even though on that particular night I was only wearing one shoe.

Later, in the deserted hall I took one last look at my photo in the final year book. Someone had crossed out the words 'most likely to succeed' and replaced them with:

'Most likely to be gunned down in a bungled liquor store hold up'.

DAILY PURSUITS

I remember a time, not so very long ago, back when man was still finding his feet, living in caves and doing it tough. Every day and night pursued by predators.

How times have changed. Now, man lives in the lap of luxury. Penthouse suites, luxury saloon automobiles, plasma screen televisions, hi-tech security systems, hand guns, all the trappings of our up-to-the-minute lifestyle.

Every day and night pursued by creditors.

GOOD FRIENDS GOOD

My friends were always around me. They always made a special effort when I was down or a little blue. Never did they arrive at or depart from my house without hugging and or kissing me.

Some cooked me exquisite food, others poured wine for me. A band of them pitched in when my house needed mending. All the time they smiled and encouraged me. They always made me welcome at their homes. Some repaired my clothes, others took turns at brushing my hair, still others waited their turn to apply ointment they had prepared for my scalp.

Never for a moment did I take any of this for granted; in return I tried to be the best friend to them that I could. I am in no way comparing myself to Jesus but my friends seemed to almost worship me as my disciples!

Never did they pester me or become overbearing, they just filled my life with the joy of their presence and friendly devotion. I often stopped and said to myself, "My cup truly runneth over".

At one particular sunny afternoon gathering, as once again my cup was running over, I called to my friends for their attention. And it was duly given to me. I wanted to ask them something that had been troubling me for some time. It was not as to why they devoted themselves to me the way they did, I would never be so crass as to ask that. No, I was intrigued to find out why my friends lived such impoverished lives, why they stuck to their mundane existences. Who did they think was going to look after them later in life?

There was silence for a moment then they broke into a raucous laughter. "Great" I thought, "they think this is one of my funny jokes". I implored of them that this was not the case, my question was in all honesty.

There was silence again, then one stood forward as a spokesperson.

"You!" he said, "you will. For this is what you told each and every one of us."

"Years ago." Another added.

"Was I drunk?" I asked them.

"Yes." Came the unanimous reply.

"But you were always drunk." someone chimed in, "You were drunk but still you told us, you said – 'Listen to me my dear friends, for though I be intoxicated by all manner of beverages, I want you to hear my slurrings and take them to heart. As my friends, my devoted friends, I want you not to fear for your collective futures. Do not grumble at your humble lives as we move forward. For I have here a notebook, a book of all my great and wonderful ideas. And I shall ply and trade these ideas in return for many great riches and these riches shall not be for one man alone. No, these riches shall be bestowed and shared amongst all whom I call friends.'

Those words reverberated and stung my ears, they sounded very much like my words and definitely my grammatical structure. Oh dear, that book, I remembered that notebook. Where the hell had I put it after all those years?

Believe me I tore the place apart until I found it, and the contents pained me in so many ways.

So many of my abandoned plans that someone else came up with years later and proved to be a winner. So many theories that proved to be correct and I had not acted upon them. Many thoughts, ideas and projects now superseded or adapted by someone else.

Oh why oh why did I not go ahead and produce that animated sitcom series I wrote about a dysfunctional nuclear family that I planned to call "The Simpkins"

HANDY TIP #1

"Remember…in a knife fight it is never handle first!"

Sternberg.

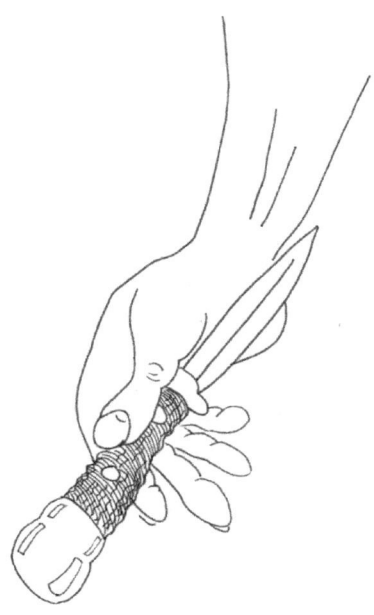

INTO THE ARMS OF MY RESCUERS

Thanks to a troublesome shipwreck I had spent several years on my own on an island. Fortunately, the waves had washed up quite a few articles from the sunken ship that I had put to good use.

A concert harp had become my bed head, an elaborate wedding dress draped over it served as a mosquito net. As time dragged by, all the men's clothing I had became tattered rags no longer fit to use. I had little choice but to take to wearing the satin night gowns that had washed up in a mahogany dresser.

The contents of a makeup box came in very handy as protection from the island's blazing sun. Also, the silk stockings helped to foil the leeches trying to attach themselves to my legs as I foraged for berries.

My back was injured in the surf the night of the ship wreck, and I found great relief in being trussed up in a corset. Thick rouge lipstick protected my lips from chaffing and splitting in the salty environment.

At night I lit every candle I had salvaged, coloured and scented, in masses around my bed so as to attract the attention of any passing ships. I was startled one night by a rowboat of sailors standing at the foot of my bed. They rescued me; and that is all they did.

That's all they did!

MONDAYS

Believe me people, it is much better to go to work with a hangover than without one.

Because as your liver and kidneys process and breakdown the alcohol and you sweat and wee it out you will gradually but surely feel better as the day wears on.

However, if you go to work sober nothing can insulate you from the sad grinding down of your remaining resolve by the ever-present stark reality that you are only going to feel worse as the day progresses.

Have a nice day!

FRINGE DWELLER

Before I grew up to be as big as I am now, I used to live amongst a crop of hair on the scalp of some kid, like a nit. Life was simple and wonderful back then. I particularly enjoyed Sunday night bath times when the kid's hair would be cleansed with uplifting fragrant shampoos and conditioners.

Winter times I would live snug under a woollen cap, in summer either shaded by a wide brim hat or hanging on tightly to strands of hair as the kid whizzed along on his brand new red bike, the summer breeze caressing his scalp.

I continued my carefree existence for a time until things started to sour for the kid. He grew up and got older and more stressed, and dandruff began to appear, in reaction to which I developed a raspy cough.

Eventually his hair became thinner and to cross from one side of his head to the other necessitated a risky dash across the barren wasteland of his cranium. Hiding in the remnants I would watch in peril as the kid's fingers scratched and rubbed at the very path I had taken. Sometimes I would sprain an ankle in an abandoned follicle.

It was a sad day the hair clippers came out for the buzz cut, and I was left on the floor amongst the ruins of my once idyllic existence. I was then faced with the daunting and chilling reality that I too must finally grow up.

RESTAURANT EXHAUST FAN

I have a favourite restaurant in town, though I can not afford to eat there all the time. If things are going rosy I can eat there once a week. If things are not going so well I have a plan, actually it's more like a secret.

I walk slowly down the lane behind the restaurant. When I am sure no one is looking I sneak under the construction site tape. Standing on the dumpster I leap onto the fire escape. Then I shimmy up the web of water pipes, gas lines and fire fighting fittings until I am on the roof next door.

From there I simply climb over a small parapet and I am on the roof of my favourite restaurant. Their roof is like a little valley amongst a sea of rooftops and sitting on it I am hidden from view.

On the roof is the 'jewel.' The outlet vent of the focaccia grill. Laying beside it out of the wind the delicious odours of garlic, sun dried tomato, feta and other exotic fare waft all about me.

I'm sure everybody has their own rooftop hiding place in the city and they are right to guard its location jealously, much like a favourite camping or fishing spot. So I am not about to divulge the **exact** location of mine.

But if you do happen to stumble upon it, the focaccia vent is the stainless steel one with the supporting cables. Not the white PVC pipe at the other end of the roof, that's the vent off the male rest rooms.

"Bon appétit!"

HOUSING

It seemed as though everyone had become addicted to houses! Everywhere, in every location, people were buying houses, building houses, renovating houses and extending houses.

As people became richer they built houses that were far too big for them. And having built those houses they went on to buy other houses. It was a sort of hobby, a sort of sport, a sort of madness.

Pretty soon the earth was covered with houses. Already people had started to build on top of one another. Low density housing became medium density which soon gave way in favour of high density which rapidly moved on to dense density housing.

The worst part was that soon the houses were built right up against the moon, and the moon became a suburb of earth. Instead of being looked at through the dreamy eyes of lovers, poets and, of course, dreamers, the moon was eyed greedily by real estate moguls.

I couldn't stand it any longer! I grabbed my tent and ran away desperately looking for somewhere to pitch it.

CHRISTMAS LUMP

Winter was approaching, and that meant Christmas would soon be upon us. Still, it seemed I was the only kid in our housing development that was well behaved, and understood the concept of manners.

The other kids delighted in misbehaviour. Threats or even a good spanking could not sway them from their misdemeanours. They bricked the chapel roof during Sunday mass. They lit paper wrapped poop on every stoop along our street. They stole and swore and bricked roofs once more. I watched from a distance and wondered why I felt so grown up.

Christmas morning came and sure enough I got my train set and just as sure every other dirty faced little urchin found a lump of coal in their tattered stockings.

All Christmas morning, on my freezing bedroom floor I tried to assemble the train set. For hours my numb fingers fumbled, trying to assemble fiddly bits of track and fence. Soon I was shivering and feeling strange.

Just before Christmas lunch I was carried downstairs and loaded into a horse drawn gig bound for the infirmary suffering from hypothermia. The camphor odoured house matron held me and vigorously rubbed the backs of my hands. I peered out from the gig and I could see the street kids. They had all pooled their coal and had made a fire in an upturned policeman's hat. They danced around it singing dirty Christmas carols, happy and warm.

The little pricks.

DAY JOB

The other night I dreamt I gave up my day job because I had at last become self-sufficient through my artwork!

I dreamt I was squatting in a neglected corner of the botanical garden where I had put my easels together and slung some spare canvas over them.

At night I warmed my toes by the flickering light of my burning sketches and pencils and dined on a deliciously coloured meal of melted crayons.

AVALANCHE

(Thredbo disaster 1997)

Half of a little ski town fell on top of itself; just gave way and rumbled down the slope burying people, other stuff and houses.

Everyone around the country stood glued to their TV set to see how it would all turn out. Would they find all the bodies? Would they find anybody alive? It went on for days, hardly anyone turned off their television. New developments were passed on at lightning speed - one of the rescuers had heard something, a faint noise beneath the rubble. Careful but furious digging ensued. People held their breath; all fingers were crossed in hope.

For some reason no one **sat** in front of their television; as a sort of mark of respect and hope everyone **stood** and faced their tv sets. It must have worked for they pulled a lucky fellow called Stewart from the pit of brick chunks and mud.

At the cafeteria at which I was the cleaner everybody clapped and cheered. My heart sank. I stood with my broom as I swept around the tables and looked towards everybody else's backs as they watched and celebrated in front of the television.

Obviously, no one was even aware that I was also trapped, buried under tonnes of twisted useless life rubble. People that worked with me, spoke with me, looked at me, none of them had any inkling of my hopeless entombment. It seemed pointless me shouting, calling out or banging above my head with a brick fragment. Pointed pieces of my life jabbed into me and people walked over me oblivious to my predicament.

It really seemed so unfair - one person gets buried alive and everyone else pitches in to help. I couldn't help but think there must be hundreds of people just as trapped as me and suffocating daily in their lives. Who was going to help us? Who was going to dig us out?

EVIL BLUE PLANET

Once there was an evil little blue planet whose inhabitants' main interest was tribal warfare. They spent much of their time and most of their money building bigger and better weapons.

Currently one of the leading brands of arms manufacturer is working on a new model that can blow up the entire world with one shot!

Above the Manager's desk and all around the munitions factory signs bear the company's slogan:

"WE'LL GET THE BASTARDS!"

LETHARGIC PIRATE

Evil man who sails the seas,
skull and cross bones in the breeze.
Leaves his undies laying around,
clean shirt never can be found.
Sails all tattered,
cannons rusty,
food all weevilly,
galley musty.
Filthy mug and greasy platter.
Hole in ship!
"aaaarrrrrhhhhh doesn't matter."

Sternberg.

FEELING ROTTEN

Apparently the rot had been setting in for some time now and I and all the others had no idea.
It wasn't until suspicion was raised, tests were done, and results came back that it was confirmed.
The rot **had** started to set in.
I wished I had gone for regular check-ups but I didn't and there was no use pondering over it.
Instead I sat in the waiting room of the clinic for people suffering rot and read the many pamphlets there:

*SO ITS ROT THAT YOU'VE GOT.
*ROT IT IS OR ROT IT'S NOT?
(Self Diagnosis Chart.)
*ROT AND HOW IT'S GOT.
*DON'T LET ROT TIE YOU IN A KNOT.
and *ROTTERS ON THE BOT.
(If you needed a personal loan.)

PROVERB

"Too many cooks may spoil the broth, but you need all the help you can get to sauté a Rhinoceros."

Sternberg.

EAST

Over in the east, in the suburb where I live, no-one is overly concerned with status or material possessions. Those that are soon sell up and move on.

The 'east', as it is known, has always been the home of railway workers and general labourers. Geographically, the east is divided into two by the rail line that runs to the large city down on the coast.

No-one, on either side of the tracks, sees themselves as better than the folks from the other side. You can visit the other side quite easily and safely anytime night or day.

The only real difference between the two halves of the east is that the other side to where I lived had a large white stallion that roamed the streets, laneways and parks. The majestic beast had been around the area for years. No-one knew where it had come from or even where it slept at night.

It was just accepted that he existed. It was seen as somewhat of a blessing to wake and find the stallion's hoof prints in your yard

I myself had seen the mighty horse on several occasions. Once he was grazing on some new shoots of grass that were growing around an old abandoned sedan. Our eyes met, then the stallion reared up and cantered off toward the sports oval in almost slow motion.

Sightings of the stallion were not rare, but everyone felt privileged from a sighting, even more privileged if he left you something to help you out with your vegie' garden.

HIGH ABOVE THE MOON

Once I was riding a wave high above the moon, way up amongst the stars, when I was joined by two laughing angels.

Smugly I asked them "Are you laughing because you've never seen this done before?"

"No," they chuckled "We are laughing because we've seen how hard these waves come crashing down!"

DEAD SEA SCROLLS

When I heard that a grotty little shepherd boy had unearthed the dead sea scrolls and ran with them to the tent of his father I was gutted.

Gutted and furious.

Furious because I myself had been playing in those very caves only weeks before. Only thing I found folded up and stuffed behind a rock was a girlie magazine. A real beauty though, in pretty good nick.

I also ran home, but I kept my find hidden from the world in the barn loft where I studied it for weeks to come. In some photos you could see the entire length of the ladies stockings! In others you could follow the lace outline of their brassieres. I ogled at every silky satin fold of those blouses, oh my stars.

Then that goat herder boy shows up, finds the scrolls, and earns himself a place in history. And the scrolls find themselves in controlled atmosphere museum space.

And me, I got nothing.

I haven't even got the girlie mag anymore on account of I can't remember who I loaned it to and I never got it back from them.

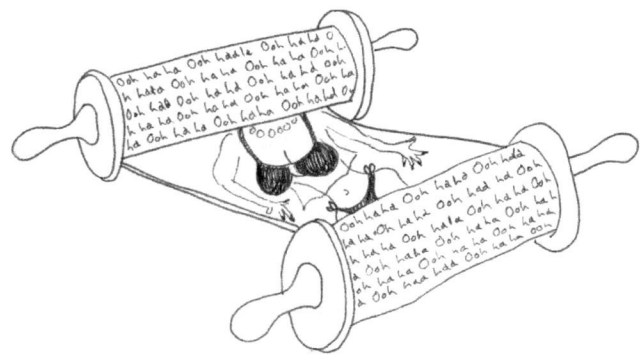

HOUSE HUSBAND

It was only early into my role as house husband but already one thing had impressed me, and that was the colour, movement and hum of the supermarkets. All manner of articles could be got there.

However, there was also all sorts of trickery to entice me to purchase items I may not have needed and of this I was constantly wary. Honesty was missing in this retail environment.

Not at all like the supply stores I used to frequent along the Ivory Coast during the time I served as a colourful macaw for the captain of a smuggler's sloop. The stores there had wooden floors and lazy turning ceiling fans. The cosy stores there smelt of canvas, hessian and hemp rope. Also available were Cuban cigars, English gin, fresh pineapples and sweet smelling oranges.

Most times sandal wood, leathery meat treats and

scrimshawed ivory were also stocked. If you needed a new spider monkey they had them too.

But getting back to the list of what I needed:
- bleach
- fluorescent light tubes
- frankfurts (low toxin)
- deodorant (extra aluminium)
- blue seas tuna (now with 10% less dolphin).

NO WARNING

Please don't warn me about anything!

For I find that pre-warned is pre-worried. If the person I am about to meet has a big nose, or a huge mole between their eyes, or they are sensitive about their lack of height or teeth, please don't warn me.

Whatever the situation, I would rather handle it in the moment, on my own, using my tact, decorum and diplomacy.

Weeks before an upcoming family reunion I was constantly being warned of Lord Langley's ballooning size and his sensitivity to it. I became so paranoid about it that at the family gathering I avoided Langley at every chance. But of course the inevitable happened, we were allocated our seats for supper and I was placed right alongside him.

"Ah, Lord Langley," I stammered then continued, "You're…eating well…I trust?"

DOG ATTACKS

There had been a spate of dog attacks down our way.

Jonesy had his calf bitten by a pit bull, Jacko received lacerations from an over-sharpened Doberman, and a ferocious team of Jack Russels dragged flimsy Johnson from his dragster bike while on his paper round.

And me?, well the street bully rubbed his abrasive Poodle, quite vigorously, right onto my sunburn!

OTHER PEOPLE'S NAMES

Surely it can't be that hard to remember other peoples names and yet civil and pleasant folk, like you and me, have trouble with remembering people's names on a daily basis.

In what seems an amazingly self-centred act, I have remembered my own name for most of my life, yet I cannot seem to show the same common decency to a newly met stranger. I can't seem to remember **their** name any longer than three seconds into the preliminary exchanging of pleasantries.

I am sure it wouldn't be that difficult to remember my new friend's name, if only I wasn't so preoccupied, my mind racing with all the truly fantastic, exhilaratingly and entertaining facts about myself that I am just bursting to tell my new acquaintance.

If only they would hurry up with the mundane dribble about what their name is and let me get started!

DOCUMENTS

We used to talk about all sorts of topics around our lunch table at work. Everyone had an opinion, and was welcome to it. Sometimes we agreed, other times not. Never, though, did it ever come to blows.

On one occasion the conversation somehow got around to time travel, the pros and cons thereof.

I was given a guarantee by one fellow that there was no need for concern as time travel would never come about. He went so far in his conviction as to give me a written guarantee. Respectful of his opinion I accepted the document.

Now a document as important as that needed extreme care taken of it, so on returning home, I opened my filing cabinet and placed it gently into the area of written guarantees.

It took its place alongside all the other guarantees made over time: the world is flat, man will never walk on the moon, it would be impossible to break the sound barrier and Elvis is dead!

Oh, and the one for the toaster.

EVIL EMPIRE

The construction of my evil empire was progressing nicely and no-one from the authorities or appropriate agencies had any inkling of its existence or intentions.

I was pleased with how everything was going smoothly and under projected budget for the start-up period. The covert recruitment drive had gone exceedingly well, bringing to the fore many ruffians, ne'er-do-wells and fiends that fitted my empire's personnel requirements wonderfully. Men with a dark past but a bright future. There were also talks in the underground pipeline of securing a band of the Beagle Boys nephews that was looking promising.

But loose lips sink ships and the unravelling began.

It seems that one of my stooges, hoons, cronies or henchmen had let something slip as they drank down at the Nemesis Lounge, a well-known haunt for hoodlums, evil geniuses and goons .... and a great place for networking.

Before I knew it my hideaway was overrun with an elite tactical response team, their superiors making straight toward the tarpaulin covering my 'chemical infusion sonic death ray device.' They measured the length and girth of my pride and joy (the death ray device) and promptly issued me with a citation-it was over legal size. And I did not have a permit to operate such a device in this precinct that is zoned semi-industrial.

I was hit with a huge fine that I was only just able to pay after selling off all my stores of enriched plutonium. A bigger insult was yet to come, as I had to undertake hundreds of hours of community service.

There I was planting trees, painting over graffiti and standing behind the counter of a downtown soup kitchen slopping up beef and barley broth to the very people I had planned to vaporise or enslave!

There seems to be no incentive for the little guy these days. What would the government have preferred that I do? Sit at home on my backside watching daytime television turning into an obese dullard and and collecting unemployment benefits? Where is the incentive and reward for people prepared to have a go?

THE FINAL GUN

For years I toiled with simple honest tools. Shovel, pick, wheelbarrow and sturdy boots.

I moved about from land to land visiting each little town and province where a simple ceremony would take place. I would be greeted by the Mayor and his dignitaries then all the townsfolk and people from the outlying districts would come forward and deposit their firearms and munitions into my barrow.

A cheering crowd would then escort me out of town.

When finally on my own I would choose a suitable site, usually a far-flung field beside a lonely stand of trees, where in the twilight I would dig a deep hole and bury all the weapons.

But this night was special! For on this night I was burying the world's last gun. My years of toil had come to an end.

As I packed down the last few clods of soil I sank to my knees relieved and contented. I held my battered old shovel in my calloused hands and gave a satisfied sigh at the thought of how quiet it would be tomorrow.

USELESS SHOVEL

And so I trudged wearily but happily back home. I had buried the world's final gun and today was the sweet tomorrow.

Before long I passed farmer Tweed and in his hands was his old shot gun, "Hey what goes on?" I implored of him. "A few weeks after you left," he replied "a fox started marauding my chickens!"

Further along the road I found other folks armed. "We brought in our harvest and we didn't like the way our greedy neighbours were eyeing our stores," they said.

All along the route to my cabin others told me of similar stories, it seemed as though there was not a gun left in the ground. I stumbled and tumbled down the track toward home, sweat and tears running down my face and hitting the dusty ground. Exhausted, I hit the ground also.

As I slept my mind whirled in a feverish dream and I found myself questioning "Surely I haven't once again busted my gut, wasted my time and got absolutely bloody nowhere?"

ON THE BOW

(Some instructions to follow)

High in the hills, lay on the ground and pretend to be on the 'bow' of the planet much like DiCaprio was on the bow of the ship in the movie of the Titanic.

Make sure there are no structures higher than you on the hill, like trees, fire lookouts, rock cairns or prayer flags, as they will detract from the experience for you.

You must be the highest thing on the hill, **you** must be the first object between the leading edge of the world and the face of space.

Dig your heels in and with your hands pull the earth tightly up against your back as it turns silently in space. Feel the immense planet beneath you as you slowly spin.

Ride the planet. Fly it.

Feel like you're the king of the world!

Of course, lose your grip on the bow of a ship and

you will have a jolly task trying to get back on. Lose your grip on the world however and you've really got your work cut out for you.

WHALE FISHING

"The most difficult procedure in whale fishing is threading the plankton on the hook!"

Sternberg.

RENOVATING MY TEETH

Everyone had heard the controversy about teeth fillings that had been made from a cocktail of compounds which were subsequently deemed to be potentially lethal.

Some fillings were of low grade plutonium others mercury and asbestos coated I seem to recall were cheapest. They were at the time, looked upon as being great wonders of medical science, just like good old wholesome lead injections.

As a consequence it was thought it would be best to have them out and replaced with porcelain fillings.

And that is precisely what I had done, it cost me a bomb, but how can you put a price on peace of mind and good health?

During a period of convalescing from dental appointments I caught up with some daytime television. Much to my horror, the story was just breaking as to where the shonky dental industry had been procuring all of this now sought after porcelain. From all the discarded porcelain toilet bowls thrown out during the recent renovating era, when every old bathroom was torn down and refurbished.

Dentists everywhere were being arrested and receiving large penalties. I'm telling you it left a very bad taste in my mouth.

BOAT THAT FLOATS

And so it finally came about that I got the very real urge to own a boat.

I had wondered most of my adult life why owning a boat had never interested me, and I often pondered when, if ever, the boat urge would come. Then out of the blue, while gazing blankly at the overflowing kitchen sink, I suddenly craved for a boat.

I wanted nothing fancy or outlandish, just something that would float basically. Seaworthy though, and something I could paint. A simple boat without complex rigging, even simpler than 'the old man and the sea boat' and easier to pull through weeds than the African Queen.

It had to be the sort of boat that I could fall in love with but at the same time a boat that wouldn't embarrass my children.

A floating-on-the-bay-at-night boat, with a canopy and coloured party lights strung upon it.

A pull-it-up-on-the-sand and sleep-in-it boat.

A glass-bottom see-through boat, or one from which we could dangle a strong light into the dark night sea and attract fish to the glow.

A satisfy-my-urge boat.

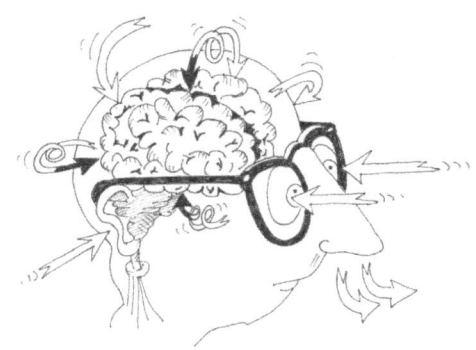

WHERE IDEAS COME FROM

Ideas usually enter the brain through the eyes or ears via some visual or aural stimuli. Once inside, the idea retreats straight toward the rear of the brain and lodges in the Area of Contemplation. It will only pass through this area once during its entire existence, hence the term, giving an idea the 'once over'.

Passing then to the Area of Reasoning, which is constructed of micro nodules, it bounces around in random fashion from one nodule to the next until it's ready to be passed on for further development. The action inside the nodule chamber gives us the phrase 'tossing the idea around.'

Having got this far the idea then goes through the centre of the brain where it is injected with enthusiasm, fired with faith, strengthened with resolve and flavoured with imagination causing belief in the idea to be heightened.

By now we have reached the top of the brain and have done so quite rapidly; this generates a fair amount of heat, causing the owner of the brain to be flushed with excitement and hot with expectation.

However, before the idea can be expelled out of the mouth in the form of "Oh I've got an idea." it must filter down through the smallest yet most powerful sector of the brain, the microscopic FEAR NUB!

Here the idea will be asked this question: "What if someone laughs at me?" Usually this is enough to send the idea shooting up into the Gland of Procrastination which is located in the front of the brain just above the nose.

An overwhelming number of ideas held in the Gland of Procrastination simply dry up. A build up or back log of ideas is thought in some schools of psychology to lead to depression. However, in a normal healthy person the Gland of Procrastination senses the irritation and secretes a green gooey substance that encases the now crusty old idea and carries it down through the nose depositing it just above the nostril rim.

The index finger removes the dried contents from the nostril rim. It is then wrapped in a sort of tissue paper and placed into a kind of porcelain bowl, not for safe keeping or dissection but for disposal.

So, there you have it, ideas start out with a flush of enthusiasm and end up with…well you get the picture.

Footnote.
Any ideas that make it out through the mouth, more often than not, enter someone else's ear as stimuli and

are stolen from the original brain, sometimes creating a small fortune for the owner of the receiving brain! In some schools of psychology this is thought to bring on depression in the original brain.

BROKEN RULE

I knew about the 'Golden Rule of the Bush' from a very early age as I was the sort of child to absorb wisdom. And yet it took me years and years of my adult life to realise that I had been breaking that very same rule for quite some time.

The 'Golden Rule of the Bush': "As soon as you realise you are lost, **stay put**, don't keep blundering along getting more and more lost. You will be easier to find if you just **stay put**."

I had been 'lost' in my life for years. I was truly in the 'bewilderedness.' And yet I blundered on and on, going around and around in meaningless circles.

What I should have done in my life was to sit down - sit down and wait. Sometime, sooner or later, someone may have found me sitting there despondent and quivering.

Then again maybe they wouldn't have tracked me down, so feeble were the paths I left behind.

LUNAR

Everybody gets excited around times of full moons, solar and lunar eclipses and so on. I know I do. And I think back to what our ancient forbears must have experienced watching them.

But this upcoming phenomenon was to be totally awesome. The moon was to pass as close to the earth as it had ever done in the history of the human race.

As usual, the electronic media covered all aspects of the upcoming event covering every angle, giving opinions and, of course, any warnings the authorities felt prudent to make. It was perfectly safe to view the moon with the naked eye it was felt, however, and they could not stress the next point enough, the observer must **NOT** under any circumstances try to touch the moon on its nearest pass!

Well, I had made **my** mind up. The day before the event I packed a few camping things together and strapped them to my pushbike. I told no-one of my plans or destination and I headed off alone to Mt Beckington.

Mt Beckington was the tallest hill of the ranges that surrounded our small township. On top of Mt Beckington was a lone tree, taller than any other in the entire district. It was up this tree that I waited for the moon.

Darkness fell, as did the temperature, I pulled my woollen hat down over my ears, and as I did the moon floated over the horizon. I could not believe my eyes, the moon was huge, white, round and cratery.

It seemed to take forever to reach my tree but when it did, I was going to do more than reach up and touch it, I was going to leap on.

And there I was at last, clinging to the moon as it sailed silently over the countryside. The view was amazing as the moon reflected light for miles ahead of its orbit. I could hear traffic below, I could hear cows, and every now and then I could hear people with their excited children watching the moon go past. "There goes another one!" I heard them shout. Another what? I remember thinking at the time.

I soon found out much to my chagrin, as I strolled around the moon, that for company I had every other irresponsible halfwit and no-hoper, every other ne'er-do-well, dim-witted fool, and idiot who just could not help themselves.

Those who could not be told 'don't reach for the moon'. 'DON'T TOUCH'.

Every other numbskull and moron, and I was marooned on the moon with them! What could I do? Become their leader?

FAIR GO MATE

So adept had I become at my chosen craft that I had received a letter from the Department of Fair Go Mate in which they implored me to 'ease up on my contemporaries'.

HOW RICH?

During my lifetime I became so amazingly wealthy that eventually I was able to afford a property that overlooked God's garden.

From the windows of one of my kitchens I would sometimes see God strolling about in the early evening, assessing his garden, checking that everything was in order, then retiring for the night. I will be honest; I did not live close enough to see His face but you could tell it was Him.

Now I did not take these sightings for granted and I know full well that it would have made a huge impact on a lot of people's lives to catch a glimpse of their God, but I must have missed out on seeing Him many more times, simply because of the need for me to be at my computer trading stocks and surveying my empire. But well, time is money.

And no, I never spoke to God over the fence and I sure as heck never threw grass clippings over His back fence either!

IMAGINE THAT

I guess that we all had an imaginary friend at some stage in our childhood.

I actually had an imaginary aunty that I used to stay with sometimes. She lived in a black three-story imaginary house in a horse paddock on the edge of town.

I loved being in her house at night, as dozens of candles tried their best to light the dark, luxurious décor. Drapes, tapestries and carved mahogany gargoyles swayed and flickered as draughts and breezes seeped through the thin, make believe walls, threatening the candelabras.

Glass beads and crystal goblets sparkled, as they shone watery shadows onto the purple and maroon wallpaper. I would lay on the deep pile carpet and drift off to sleep. Her voice seemed far away as she lifted me into that huge brass bed and billowing eiderdown.

Yes, those visits were among the best things that I ever imagined as a kid.

PRETTY PRINCESS

Once there was a princess whose beauty so enchanted the people that they felt they could never have enough images of her.

However, no-one fully understood the impact that all of this image taking was having on the princess's soul. Then all at once, at midnight, in the most romantic city in the world, her soul was whisked away and the image left behind was that of her crumpled carriage.

ISLANDS

As a kid I dreamt that when I grew up I would live on an island, surrounded by crystal clear ocean.

Much later in life I realised that no matter where you lived on this planet, itself an island in an ocean of space, you are living an island existence.

Your home, no matter how ramshackle, is your own island, surrounded by a cold sea of strangers, an ocean of everybody else.

And you leave your island and travel that sea at your own peril. For as sure as there be tides and waves and howling gales, the ocean outside your door is every fathom as dangerous as the real sea. And many people, like me, travel in vessels that are far from seaworthy.

WHEN?

"Oh, when will I ever learn?"
"For all the vigorous rubbing of my life against the harshness of reality all I have ever achieved is an increase in my mortal friction!"

Sternberg.

ROCKET FUEL

I blundered into a clearing way out in the bush and was startled by a group of aliens. They were gathering sticks, their shiny metal spacecraft parked amongst the trees.

An uneasy silence dragged on for some time. I looked at them, they looked at me, they looked at each other. I smiled, over zealously, then clamped my lips tight, what if bared teeth was an act of intimidation where they came from?

"Good morning!" I blurted, then shrank back, "Too forward" I thought, "too forward!". My mind was racing. They glanced back and forth amongst themselves, bleeping, whirring and creaking.

"Good morning." They imitated back. They all quickly pulsated as if they were giggling.

"And um…gathering sticks?" I motioned towards the baskets that they were filling. Excitedly they offered me the sticks as if embarrassed.

"No you keep them, you have them." I assured the nearest alien. They seemed grateful.

It was obvious we had a language barrier but we were all civil beings and through hand gestures, facial expressions and body language we soon had a semblance of understanding.

I pieced together from our efforts to communicate that they had, centuries ago, mastered the complex science of nanotechnology. From this they were able to manoeuvre atoms around to construct tiny but very powerful fuel cells and engines for their space craft.

"And therefore only use small amounts of nuclear power?" I guessed.

They looked at me shocked. They shook their many heads; they obviously thought I was some sort of irresponsible maniac to consider the use of nuclear power.

"What would we do with the waste?" they indicated.

They showed me that instead they had invented tiny little reactors that worked similar to wood chip heaters. By burning very small sticks in metal tubes and funnelling the heat through Nano ports into their engines they were able to streak across the universe at a very economical rate.

Our conversation started stalling so I decided to make a discreet exit. I shook one of the creature's hands, it blushed and I realised it must not have been it's hand! I backed slowly out of the clearing as the aliens scampered with their baskets of twigs back up the ramp into their ship.

I was walking briskly back toward my home when their space craft buzzed over my head then zoomed upward and shot into the heavens. The homely smell of fire smoke drifted and wafted about me. The lovely smell of dry burning twigs and gum leaves.

So much more fragrant than carbon dioxide fumes and far friendlier than enriched plutonium.

I wish we were that clever and advanced.

SELF DISCOVERY

Miles from anywhere on a pilgrimage of self-discovery, I came across a stunning, although baffling, grisly find in the stifling heat of the desert.

I had been scrambling over a field of huge red boulders when I stumbled across the skeleton of the Devil! Amazingly, it seemed he had perished out here in the harsh dry Australian outback.

For a moment I considered giving him a decent burial, I then decided against it and instead kicked his skull off.

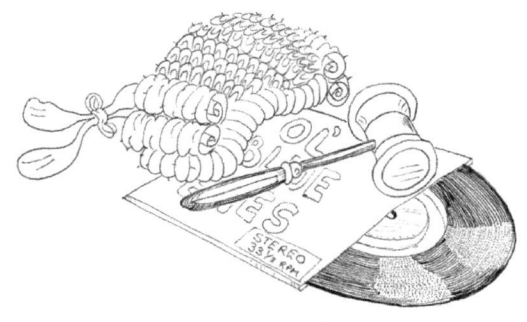

MAGISTRATE

Sometimes I used to fill in for a friend of mine who worked as a magistrate in the local courthouse, even though I was merely a janitor and not at all qualified and my friend knew it; it was just that sometimes he wanted time off and asked me to cover for him, that's what friends do.

There was an attorney there that I took a real shine to, though it was definitely not for his courtroom prowess. He was quite often late for sessions, seldom wore a suit (or indeed long pants for that matter.) Most of the time his addresses to the jurors or the bench weren't even relevant to the case at hand. He also had the habit of delaying the start of hearings by laying on the courtroom floor while listening to his collection of Frank Sinatra records through a set of headphones.

He would sing along out of tune to Frank quite oblivious to the disgruntled objections from the opposing attorneys.

"Objection overruled!" I would bellow as I banged down my friend's gavel. "Let him listen to one more song."

I don't know why I tolerated his childish unprofessional behaviour, I guess it was because he reminded me so much of myself.

SCRABBLE LEGEND

In all my years of playing scrabble I have heard tell of the mysterious and seldom seen letter, double apostrophe X, which I am led to believe looks like this: X".

So rare and valuable is this strange consonant that if it is produced and used during a game of scrabble the game comes to a temporary standstill while the current value of the letter is assessed.

The value can be tracked daily on the stock market page of large metropolitan broadsheet newspapers or after hours stockbrokers have access to an ancient abacus that can be used to estimate the current value to the third decimal point!

Rarely, though, do serious scrabble players go to such lengths to assess the value of the double apostrophe X for it is considered poor form and it is proper etiquette just to accept that if it is used against you then you are well and truly beaten.

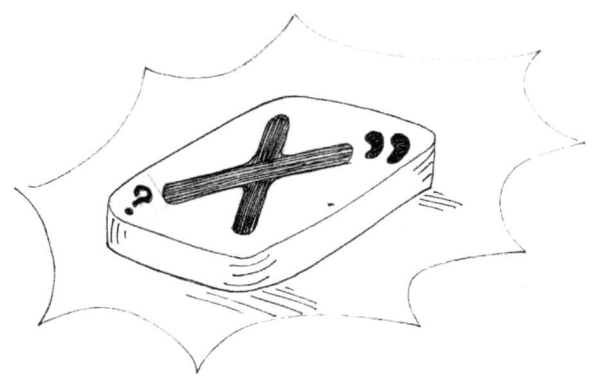

QUINCE TREE

A quince tree had grown on the very site where dad and I had camped more than twenty years before.

I remember dad cutting up a quince from our hamper to eat around our campfire that night. I forced myself to eat several of the tart, furry quince wedges so as to be like my father. Around the same period of my childhood I had persevered to acquire the taste for black tea the same way my father drank his, a kind of tribute based on the admiration I had for him. An admiration that I felt every boy should have for their own father.

And now a twenty year old quince tree stood in memory of one of our old camp sites. How well it had done considering the simple ceremony that surrounded the planting of it's seeds. I remember how dad had dug a hole with his boot heel, dropped in the core and splashed in the last of his black tea from his enamel mug.

Fancy that, the seed had sprouted, grown and thrived

and I had never returned to see its progress in all that time. The tree must have endured dry spells, storms, sunny days and hail. Bearing fruit for nobody or one or two passing tramps.

I envied that fruit tree in a way. How amazing it must have been living on that hill, seeing the summer storms rolling in across the ranges, having the scented breeze caress it's summertime leaves, sleeping during the winter cold as the rain hammered down all around. I wondered if the nights had been as magical for the tree as they had been for my father and I around our little fire, listening to the owls hooting to one another across the valley, now and then hearing an old mountain ash crashing through the smaller trees as it fell to the ground. I had no idea what storms the tree had endured in my twenty year absence.

Of course the quince tree had no idea of the storms I had endured either, and in comparison I seemed far more gnarled and twisted and with a fair amount of moss growing on my south side.

THE THIRD EAR

The back of my neck had been persistently itchy and no amount of rubbing or scratching eased it. None of my moisturisers, creams, emollients, balms or soothing salves had any perceivable effect.

I tramped from medical practitioner to Chinese herbalist but to no avail. Many a specialist sniffed and scraped at my nape but all came up empty handed, except of course for their exorbitant fee! Until one Dermatologist I was referred to called on the opinion of a 'Futurist.' Together they conducted thorough tests on my person, then sent me home as they sifted through the data.

What they came up with had them very excited indeed. It appeared that I wasn't victim to a rash, fungal infection, worm, tropical disease, bacteria, hex or curse but in fact was in the early stages of evolution!

They surmised that as the Information Age gathers pace and careens toward lightspeed, two ears will not be enough to absorb all the information and that, as a consequence, mankind will evolve a third ear (actually an antenna) And it seemed that this was exactly the sensation I was experiencing - the very embryonic twitching of evolution.

The medical world, in fact the entire world, could not get enough of me: the 'Evolution Man'. I was paraded before an assortment of panels and review boards, subjected to a myriad of testing and assessments, and was the subject of endless interviews within the electronic media. I was flavour of the month.

Right up until the moment I cracked under the strain of the spotlight and of constantly being asked the question: "What is it like being at the very start of an evolutionary process?"

"What's it like?" I blurted angrily, "I'll tell you what it's like mate. It's real F@#**ing itchy that's what it's like!"

MATHS

I have just about had a gut full of those morons who continually poke fun at algebra.

Inevitably it's these jerks who do not carry the X and fail to square root the Y and find themselves in all sorts of conundrums.

Then it's left up to people like you and me with our algebraic sensitivities to leap to their rescue and save their dopey '2+2 mentality' driven backsides!

MY SUIT

How strange. The news report of a suit found floating in the ocean. It was a secluded beach along the Queensland coast and it was an entire suit still on the hanger – jacket, pants, shirt, tie, the lot!

I thought very little of it, until several days later when I was contacted by the Harbour Police to identify the suit. Their Investigators believed it to be mine. And it was!

How strange. How could my suit have gotten to Queensland, where I had never even been? How did it reach that remote beach, and how did it get into the water?

For the next week everywhere I went for coffee people at the other tables were talking. "How could someone let that happen to their suit?" they asked each other. "Obviously so rich he has more suits than he would ever need, so what if one suit downs in the ocean."

"Yes, obviously an uncaring sort of rich bastard, fancy

not taking better care of your suit, especially so close to water." And so it went on.

No, no, they were wrong. I have never been rich and I've only ever had two suits, one now water damaged. I hardly ever have cause to wear them, you know the sort of occasions, weddings, funerals, court appearances, that type of thing.

How could people be so wrong about me?

How easily people can get the wrong impression.

How strange.

SITUATIONS VACANT

Look, I came real close to getting that job at NASA and I know at which point of the interview I lost it.

Someone on the interview panel asked me, "How do you think you will get on at NASA in the area of promotional prospects?" To which I replied, "Well it's my assumption you don't have to be a rocket scientist to do well here mate." It was at about this point that one fellow on the assessment panel seemed to take it real personal. "No," he said "no you do! You do have to be a rocket scientist here!"

After that, the tone of the interview was more or less that I had not, in fact, done enough research into NASA and what it hoped to achieve in the market place.

And while they never said it in as many words, I got the overwhelming impression that it was one of those try-again-next-time type scenarios.

MY WAR TIME PARTICIPATION

During most of the wars I had my own calico tent office down a lane, off the main street of tents that were home to the Generals, War office liaison staff and assorted officers. A hand scribbled sign above the entrance to my tent told of my strategic speciality.
    'HASTY RETREATS BEATEN.'

TAKING YOUR OWN LIFE

Only you can take your own life and change it for the better and I suggest you do it now, just as I have done.

Go out into the shed or under that tree in the yard and take your own life by the scruff of the neck and shake the living daylights out of it.

Really get a good grip; now shake!

Make sure you have your life's undivided attention by giving it a cuff over the ear hole like this, "THWACK!"

Now take your own life by the shirt collar and by the belt round its pants, wrestle it around so that your life is now facing the bright sunny future.

Now with a short run up, boot your own life fair up the backside!

MY DNA

On the overhead projector they showed me an image of my DNA. This was my biological blueprint they said. It programmed how I was to be, my hair, my hair colour, my height, weight, looks, skin problems, medical conditions, athletic ability, baldness, likes and dislikes.

But sadly, after extensive testing, they found no evidence of success in my genetic makeup. The best I could hope for was rancid failure.

The test cost $1800.00, none of it claimable through the Government's pharmaceutical benefits scheme.

TIMBER TALK

I prefer the language of years ago when words were made of wood. Not just any old wood either, but teaks, mahogany and ebony, intricately carved and adorned with metals or strengthened with cast iron.

Not like the flimsy, wispy conversations of today with no wood to be heard anywhere.

Not even warped pine, chipboard or MDF.

Words today barely even exist. They are typed onto computer screens and become virtual ghosts of themselves, their hard copy hidden in electronics too small for the human eye to see. Modern conversations don't stay true, words or whole sentences shifted around or deleted altogether at the touch of a plastic button.

Years ago, it could take people days to construct a single sentence using carefully chosen words and proper grammar, with every letter and word carved in wood. Things that you said stood and men stood by their words of wood. Today I curse those stupid text messages and emails I receive all the time through the air or fibre optic cables.

Well I will soon be getting even with those stupid message senders.

I have sent them all a message and it's on its way even as we speak. I sent it two days ago and they should receive it sometime next month. It's carved from river red gum, edged with iron and being carted on a wagon pulled by two massive Clydesdale horses. The message reads as follows:

"GET STUFFED!"

NICE COOL BREEZES

It was one of those stifling summer nights where you drift in and out of a disturbed sleep. Where you are troubled by weird dreams until you wake with a jolt.

I awoke one side of midnight, on which side I wasn't sure. Something had happened, the breeze had changed. It was definitely cooler but there was something else that I couldn't quite put my finger on. Then it dawned on me; this was the exact same breeze that had blown on me many years ago back in 1973.

I was wide awake now but still the night felt dream like.

This was the very same breeze that had caressed and tickled me way back then. I held my face toward it and breathed it in. I wondered where this breeze had been all these years. Where had it been blowing since that night on the coast? Three friends and I had been sleeping in my old station wagon down on the beach, two of us in the back, one on the front seat and another had his bed set up on the roof rack. "Under the stars," he had said.

Man, I wish they were all still alive so I could phone them to come and feel this breeze again. It would have been futile waking my wife, or my children, as they wouldn't understand that this was the exact same breeze I had felt before.

So I got up, put on an old pair of denim jeans that were cut down into shorts, the height of swimwear fashion back in our day, and sat on the step of the French doors. I closed my eyes and let that breeze swirl all over me.

I could smell the vinyl of my old station wagon's interior and could faintly hear the melody of the Pink Floyd tape we had been playing that night.

Later, my wife found me upside down on our bed smiling and mumbling to myself, "Oh yeah, 1973."

THE CRUEL SYSTEM

Two years short of qualifying for the old age pension, my frail grandfather had to apply for welfare benefits. Unfortunately this meant he had to accept any jobs that the agency found for him.

A position **was found for him**, as member of a band of pugilists that toured the outback rural areas of Australia as part of a travelling show. The fighters took on any volunteers from the crowd and bets were placed. My grandad the poor old bugger, got dragged around the Northern Territory, sweltering in the heat and getting the living daylights belted out of him for months.

But what could he do? If he turned down the job he would have had his benefits cut or severely reduced. He had to take it!

Eventually, via his own endeavours, he landed a position posing as a corpse for insurance scams.

MOON SWINGS™

Remember those fad toys of your childhood? One in particular that I longed for was THE MOON SWING™. Some boffin at NASA had designed it. It did not need a tree branch or any other structure to hang from, like a regular child's swing. Once you had worked out the lunar co-ordinates the swing would be suspended in mid-air, held aloft by the gentle pull of the moon!

I held little hope of ever owning a MOON SWING™ as my parents were not rich and were quite sceptical of 'newfangled gadgets'.

Memories from my childhood are hazy but somehow a MOON SWING™ did find its way into our house. I do remember my father (the sceptic) poring for hours over the blueprints that were used for factoring the moon's gravitational pull zones.

I stood beside my father outside in the yard on the many nights that followed. He grappled with the swing and the map and the lists of co-ordinates; eventually we got the swing to hover but alas it was directly over the only concreted area of the yard. Mum thought it too dangerous to swing there.

The next night the swing hung so close to the back fence as to leave no room for swinging.

Next night, the same thing only this time it was up against the garden shed.

Two nights later it would only hang over dad's pride and joy, the rhubarb patch; definitely no swinging there.

Time went by and the swing never ventured out from the broom closet where it was kept and junk gradually gathered around it.

Some time later, while I was searching the house for old coins, I looked in the dim broom closet. The MOON SWING™ had gone.

I never found out what happened to it.

Dad had either taken it back to the shop, or 'burned the bastard', or chopped it up, or had thrown the thing to blazes. All things **he had** threatened to do.

OLD NOTE BOOK

Recently, I was rummaging through some of my old items when I found a battered old note book. It had all sorts of stuff in it. Including something I had written in my early twenties, and which I had forgotten all about.

I then remembered that I was prompted to write it after being told many times by teachers, parents, girlfriends, work mates and others to "GROW UP."

In that old book I had written detailed plans on exactly how I was going to grow up, the very path I would take, and the example I would set.

No more silly songs, dirty poems, crazy voices, ridiculous dances, day dreaming, or drawing stupid pictures. I would cut my hair, shave, bathe, wear respectable clothes, have proper employment, make sound investments, maintain relationships – all sorts of great stuff.

But I had forgotten all about it!

I mulled over the old pages of that note book for ages,

resigned to the fact that it was too late for them to do me any good now but oh how I wish I had stuck to those plans.

SWEATY DREAMS

I had no idea that I was dreaming but it should have been painfully obvious. Not only had I managed to pull front row seats for a new tv show entitled 'Real Naked Ladies' but I had also landed the enviable task of hosting the show!

So there I was in studio No1, my heart pounding with anticipation, microphone in hand when the curtain lifted and the theme music for the show started blaring over the speakers.

The theme music seemed strangely familiar to me, I listened to it intently and even started to hum along to it. Then the penny dropped. It was the same music my alarm clock plays, CRAP. It was my alarm clock!

I sat bolt upright in bed with three things becoming clear to me:

a) I was only dreaming.
b) I was late for work.

c) There was no show on any network called 'Real Naked Ladies.'

So in my disappointment I thought, "I won't go to work at all today, I'll call in sick later in the morning," and so I fell back to sleep where I dreamed I was the host of a tv show called 'Real Knackered Ladies.'

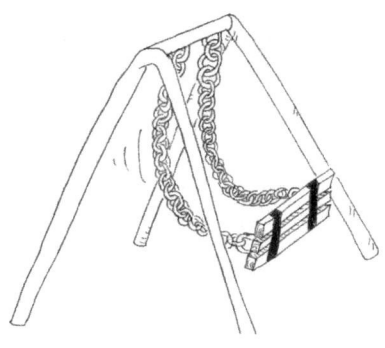

PRENUP'

It had reached the point where my wife would no longer tolerate me passing wind in our matrimonial bed. Nor would she put up with me blowing off in the bedroom per se, reminding me of my prenuptial promise only to enter the sanctum of her bedroom to worship her. Neither would she allow me to partake in the act of flatulence in the lounge, kitchen, hallway, bathroom or laundry. Out of bounds also was the front foyer (in case of unexpected guests arriving shortly thereafter).

Even if I stood outside in the yard to relieve the pressure she would be tapping on the window above the kitchen sink demanding to know what I was doing out there.

"Nothing dear." I would meekly reply before trying to persuade the dog to go for a walk with me up to the nearby park, which the dog (with its keen sense of smell) was always reluctant to do.

Inevitably I would walk to the park alone. And almost always the children playing there would run home crying out, "Mummy, mummy, the farting man is up at the swings again!"

EXPLORERS' CLUB

How proud I was as the explorers' club awarded me the annual trophy. For out of all the intrepid intrepideers, I was the most intrepidest! And deemed most likely to undertake future acts of intrepidity.

PLANS TO BLOW UP THE MOON!

Late at night I stumbled into a dark recess of the internet. I hacked into its classified section, and scrolling down I was shocked to find a file on myself. Delving further, I was horrified to find that I had once been someone else! Not in another life, but at some secret stage of this one.

I hurriedly scribbled down my last known address; a budget hotel above a chicken distillery in Little China town.

In the drizzling rain the next morning I entered the hotel. The desk clerk, half recognising me, handed over the keys to my room.

In my cobwebbed room I found everything undisturbed, as if I had left in a big hurry. I rifled through drawers and scoured the shelves.

Behind a hanging painting I found a crumpled envelope. I cleared the bedside table and switched on the lamp. Inside the envelope were folded papers detailing the plans of some sort of terrorist activities. Lists of contacts, foreign passports, NASA access codes and finally, detailed plans on how I intended to finance and engineer a plot to blow up the moon!

Apparently the plan was abandoned for several reasons. Escalating costs, internal bickering, design faults with the rocket, and growing concerns over my declining sanity. I sat on the bed bewildered, astonished, stunned and amazed.

To think, once, albeit in a secret life, I had plans.

REAL PLANS!

WHAT TO ASK FOR

Once again an angel appeared above me as I slept and she gently woke me to the night. She was inches above my face and although she spoke quietly to me her voice filled the room and sounded like a chorus of southern gospel singers.

"What would you ask for the world to have?" she cooed. I was still half asleep and not yet fully believing what I was seeing, so she repeated her question, "What would you ask for the world to have?" she whispered boomingly. I looked at my sleeping wife and the angel assured me it was only I that could hear her.

I was still somewhat confused, so my angel spoke once more. "If you could ask for the world to have anything what would it be?" I thought for a moment. The world sure did need a lot of things, many things, alas, so many things!

"Anything?" I asked my angel.

"Absolutely," she sang.

In retrospect I understand where my answer came from. I was still waking up, I was confused, bewildered and in total disbelief of the whole situation. And while I was aware that the world needed food and drinking water and peace and healing…I asked for Elvis.

I honestly asked could the world have Elvis back. Happy Elvis, when he was still fit and handsome. I promised that the world would take care of him this time and help and protect him and love him tender and keep him happy.

"Elvis," sang the angel as she left my room.

I awoke to the new day and got on with my life with no recollection of my dream or encounter, whichever it was, until later that day as I was watching the evening world news on television. It was then that all the angst and despair triggered my memory.

The world was crying out for so many things and I had asked for Elvis? I felt guilty I must confess and not just a little selfish. I had never been a big Elvis fan until sometime after his untimely passing, not until I heard about and tried to understand his situation. Terrible how someone who made so many people happy struggled with happiness themselves. I felt very sorry for him and maybe I was looking for a way of giving him and us a second chance. And who knows, with Elvis back we could have made a lot of people happy and this might have started us on a path to getting the other things the world needed.

Anyway, it was years ago that the angel asked me that question. We never did get Elvis back, and I can only assume that it was not a real encounter with an angel or to that she did not take me seriously. People often don't.

Perhaps it was like a poll and the angel asked many people that night and Elvis did not poll high enough, or maybe the angel is still counting the votes. Or it might just be that the world got something else and I missed out on seeing what that was. Maybe she wasn't a real angel.

Sometimes I wake up during the night, about the same time as my angel appeared years before and I am sobbing. As I drift back to sleep I hear myself saying "I tried Elvis, I tried."

OLD MATTRESS

Last night was the worst sleep I have ever had.

Except perhaps for that time I took delivery of a mattress constructed entirely out of marshmallow. At the time I purchased it I remember assuming how deliciously comfortable it would be.

However, on the very morning I unwrapped it, my children nibbled and licked it as I took the plastic wrapping to the recycle bin. They heard me returning and left by the French doors to escape detection, inadvertently letting in the pets. The dog and the cat wasted no time in leaping onto the unprotected mattress and licking it with great fervour.

That night I was forced to sleep on a sticky, gooey marshmallow mattress that was covered in animal hair.

The night was made even more uneasy by my uncomfortable bluestone pyjamas.

ART SMOCK

Even though I was in my middle aged years I would never commence any artistic endeavour without first putting on my art smock. Even just for writing, for some of my ideas were messy. Very messy indeed.

Muddied ideas dredged up from my sorry old past. My pen all bloodied from some notions that were much too close to my heart and, of course, other ideas that were simply crap.

FLAGGING

Here at last was my big opportunity. As the winner of an employee morale-boosting competition, I was the one to raise the company flag when the owner of the factory visited from overseas.

Unfortunately in my inexperience and youthful exuberance I had inadvertently raised the 'plague on board' flag.

The owner's limo sped back to the airport, the plant was shut down and I was set upon. Some time later I contracted a mild case of influenza.

DREAM THINGS

For some time now I have been secretly bringing back things from my dreams. I show them to no-one and I hide them in a shoebox under my bed.

Objects that were given to me by angels, demons and sometimes deceased movie stars. Trinkets, gems, clippings from strange dream foliage, tokens, ticket stubs from posthumous music concerts, ideas and instructions on how to do all sorts of 'dream only' activities.

The first things I ever brought back with me were artworks, poetry and little stories. These were shown to me by dream folk who insisted I commit them to memory. Of course I offered payment for them, but the simple people of dream town would not hear of it, and besides, my money was no good there.

ALL I COULD DO WAS LAUGH

One night the king and I stole a rocket and took it for a joy ride.
"Come back!" called the guard.
"Up yours!" bellowed the king.
Honestly, all I could do was laugh.

YETI TRAP

"Build a better Yeti trap and the world will beat a path to your yurt!"

Sternberg.

FINE

Like most of the professors, surgeons and executives at the corporation of which I am an integral part (janitor) I too had adopted burglary as a second source of income to help meet the escalating costs of my speeding fines.

Our overzealous government had seen how effective the speeding fines were at bleeding the population white in order to fund all manner of dubious art projects.

Trying to defend yourself at the scene of your commuting 'crime' was futile.

At my last 'offence' I was trying to explain to the law enforcer that I had only taken my eyes off my speedometer for a split second in order to see where I was going when he butted in with his baton, offended at my self-centred arrogant attitude and apparent total lack of respect for other road users.

WELCOME TO MY WORLD

As a kid there were two lines from a couple of songs from that era that really struck a chord with me: "Welcome to my world built with you in mind" by Dean Martin, and "We'll build a world of our own that only two can share" by The Seekers.

I used to daydream about building my own world, in fact my own planet! Hey, I was only a kid.

Before I knew it I was an adult and soon the money began rolling in. After bills and expenses I put the rest of the money toward building my own planet. I had a team of welders work on the metal frame then on my own I began cladding the sphere with timber - timber was cheaper! I used old wardrobes, fence palings, second-hand weatherboards, anything I could get my hands on.

It took years and years of my life and labours but, hey, everybody needs a hobby. Soon it was enormous. Not as big as a real planet but big enough for me.

Finally it was finished and ready for launching into it's own orbit. I packed it full of supplies and had my planet manoeuvred into the ocean. My plan was to float it to Chile in South America, for at the southernmost tip of Chile there was a suitable launching place. A long beach ran downhill for miles ending in a natural formation of rock that resembled a ramp. My plan was to roll my planet down the beach and then off the ramp, and into orbit!

I sailed my planet towards Chile and was accompanied by a flotilla of support vessels; well actually, they didn't support me as much as ridicule me, all the time bouncing empty bottles and cans off the side of my planet.

The launch beach had hundreds of onlookers, backpackers, amateur astronomers, people who chase solar eclipses and assorted other folk in search of a good laugh.

Plenty of willing helpers got my planet onto the sand and helped me bowl it down the beach toward the ramp. It built up momentum quicker than expected and bounded away from us. All I could do was watch in horror; all the onlookers could do was laugh.

How fast it was going when it hit the ramp is anyone's guess but it took off into the air just as I had planned. By the time we got to the ramp my planet was just a speck in the sky. "It's gone," I muttered in disbelief, but as we stood and watched the speck got bigger and bigger, it was coming back down! People scampered and squealed, bundling up their telescopes.

We needn't have worried, my planet burned up on re-entry. One quick flash and a few sparks then the air slowly began to fill with twisting, fluttering black embers.

People howled with laughter, their faces contorted in pain from mirth exhaustion. The remains of my planet drifted silently for miles on the breeze. All that time and effort gone and not even in a blaze of glory, just a quick flash and a few sparks.

Welcome to my world.

MY LIFE'S LIFE BOAT PT 2

I took too long to make my boat,
it didn't turn out how I'd planned it.
All the bits I had saved up,
were gone and stolen by bandits!
So in the end I had to rush it,
it turned out quite a shamble,
made of cardboard, tissue and sticks,
and powered by an anvil.

　　　　　　　　　　　　　Sternberg.

CPSIA information can be obtained
at www.ICGtesting.com
Printed in the USA
BVHW03fES42305519
549124BV00001B/109/P